The West End Boyz

"The B*tch Bit Me
And I kinda liked it"

Introduction
"Jack Weston from the west end"

Hey, If your reading this, I'm kinda
dead. don't worry my life wasn't
all that great, so I'm not gonna
bore you to death by telling you
about it, its bad enough one of us
is dead already. This story is about
how I died, why? And how I've
never felt more alive. My name is
Jack Weston and I'm from the
west end of Skyguard City, go
ahead, laugh, I heard all the jokes
before growing up so this isn't my
first rodeo, in fact the first rodeo
I've ever been to was a week ago

but thats neither here nor there. My life took a turn, for better or worse? I guess you could be the judge once you know everything; you see last week was my twenty-first birthday and like always, me and the boys were supposed to crush Valley West and make the suburbs of Skyguard our bitch, excuse my french. Plans changed though, it was last minute when one of my closest bro's said "bro, lets go to Kroxce city for your B-Day bro" how was I supposed to refuse? I mean come on the city of sin for my twenty-first birthday, what could possibly go wrong? Long story short I was like "fuck yeah bro, lets do it" next thing I knew me and my closest bro's, Donny aka D-note, Mike aka Just Mike, John boy aka John? and Shawn aka S-class, were on a private jet to Kroxce like the rich pretty thugs we were. I guess this is the part where we flash back to the day of my birthday, to find out how I died? How I'm writing this a week later? And why you would care? Good news for you, this story is totally kick ass. Bad news for me, its the story of my life or death? You get the point.

chapter 1:B-day/D-day

"Happy birthdays and R.I.P's"

 August 3rd 2018, who would have thought? The day I was supposed to be celebrating my life would end in my death. Things started out so normal waking up to the soft touch of? Not, Anastasia Wolf, who is only the hottest social media influencer in the world and girl of my dreams, literally?…Soooo, my dream was rudely interrupted by my dude Donny with some stellar news so even though, not seeing Anastasia Wolf take off her thong was a crime against humanity, dude, it was my fucking birthday.

Donny:"Bro, wake the hell up its your b-day or should I say v-day, haha, hope you lose it tonight bro"

Jack:"Dude get lost, I'm tired as shit…are you? bro are you filming me? Like bro you better not be on live!"

Shawn:"Dude, its almost 10am we should be crushing puss right now"

Mike:"Like you would know anything about crushing puss, S-class"

Donny:"Come on Mike, Shawn crushes puss all the time…Thats why his neighbor can't find her cat, hahahahahaha"

Jack:"Hahaha…Bro's,"

John boy:"Yeah bro"

Shawn:"whats up bro?"

Jack:"BROOOOOO'S"

Donny:"YEEAAH bro"

John boy:"Tell us whats up bro?"

Jack:"IT'S MY FUCKING B_DAY BROOOOOO'S!!!!!"

Happy as fuck, hashtag blessed as a mother fucker, to be twenty-one, gorgeous and rich as shit, who else would I rather be? It was my time, I was next in line of a long list of Weston men to rule the Burbs. This was my birthright, our birthright, me and my bro's, who's fathers were bro's before we were even born. We came from new money, our fathers built everything we have now from the ground up, but in the burbs of Skyguard, old money is king and growing up no one ever let us forget that. clawing our way up through the social ladder was a challenge but we made it, we were finally where we needed to be. My bro Donny was connected at birth his uncle was Cheviak Mafia from the old country, he owned a ton of clubs in Gridlock City, Kroxce City, Skyguard and Krowish City, this gave us clout seeing as we had the keys to the club scene, plus it didn't hurt that Donny is a total gangster. Mike was our ace, star athlete, fashion icon, and total chick magnet. Shawn is the princess of the group, like no joke he pampers himself more then any girl I know, total valley suffer dude, typical of West Skyguard. Even though we tease him about being a virgin its only cause somehow he's a total chick magnet that can't seem to careless about hooking up. John

Boy is a tech genius, like big headed glasses wearing level smart, so its safe to assume he's the brains of our operation. Thats my crew, my band of brothers, our birthdays only months apart mine being the last, we decided when we were all twenty-one we would invest in our dream of starting a Hip Hop, Pop, rock band, that would totally change the music industry, with me out front as the pop singer, Mike as the rap artist, Donny as our Dj and producer, Shawn as our punk rock vocalist, and John Boy as our manager and fashion designer, we built our brand on social media, The West End Boyz were the talk of the town, as the top social media influencers and people hadn't even heard our music yet. So when we were faced with the dilemma of whether or not to go to college or go into business for ourselves we chose to say fuck college and save up to do what we loved. the plan was simple, we were gonna take over the fucking world, but first we had to survive my birthday.

Chapter 2: Vegas anyone?

"A trip to remember"

   Later that day we were scheduled to shut the city down, Donny handled the clubs we would hit up and made sure there wasn't a V.I.P section anywhere in Skyguard that wasn't already booked and reserved for us. Shawn dropped the locations to his followers and like that every model slash wannabe actress in a hundred miles wanted to be wherever we were gonna be that night. Mike using his local celebrity status created a network of industry contacts, with a few phone calls we were hours away from rubbing elbows with the hottest celebrities in the game. Everything was coming together we were gonna go public with the launch of "West End Boyz" entertainment, but our resident genius had other plans.

John Boy:"Bro, lets go to Kroxce for your B-Day bro"

Jack:"dude what are you talking about we are hours away from the party of the century"

Donny:"Changing plans now would be career suicide we have nothing setup for Kroxce"

John Boy:"I disagree, we should be moving culture and controlling whats hot, so how about we show the world how badass we are by not showing up to our own launch"

Mike:"dude theres press and celebs showing up to these events, how do we bail on Them?"

Jack:"I think thats his play"

John Boy:"dam straight it is, imagine the press coverage, the West End Boyz shut down Skyguard only to stand up thousands of party goers and hundreds of celebs, think of the Social media press, photos of packed clubs all over Skyguard with empty V.I.P sections"

Donny:"we would be telling all of Skyguard we are to good for them"

Mike:"and no celeb is too big to get curved by us"

Jack:"we would be fucking krowlocks"

John Boy:"now your all getting it"

Jack:"fuck yeah bro, lets do it"

It was that simple, a short last minute conversation sealed our fates and we were off to Kroxce city. John Boy scored us a private jet from his dads collection and made hotel reservations, while Donny called in some favors at the biggest casinos in Kroxce to let them know we were coming, Mike got in touch with some local Kroxce city high rollers and let them know we wanted to have a spend off to see who could blow more cash in one night. Shawn called up an agent that works out of Kroxce he knew from the industry who guaranteed us the hottest chicks in Kroxce city would be on hand when we touched down, and sure enough when we landed twenty-five girls were waiting in the jet hanger, five girls a piece all top models and they were only the appetizers. We were in Kroxce, and we had no clue what was in store for us.

Chapter 3: Seven sins
"and so little time"

We survived the limo ride to the hotel and arrived at 7am, little did we know in 6 hours, I would be dead, but before I died we were gonna have one hell of a night. The city of sin isn't just a catch phrase, its a hundred percent true and in the next 6 hours, me and my bro's would be faced with all seven of them in the forms of seven people we probably should have avoided. A stoner/drug dealing bellhop, an Irish pimp, a crazy stripper, my ex girlfriend, a homicidal cab driver, a fortune telling waitress and a hotel maid; one of these people would end up killing me, think you know who?

Chapter 4: Sin Number 1
"Sloth & stuff"

Not soon after arriving at the hotel we encountered the first person we should have avoided, who would introduce us to the first sin of the night, his name was Colby aka light bulb the bellhop at the hotel. It all started when he asked to help us with our bags, we wanted to say no considering we didn't have anything except a few backpacks but that would be totally awkward so we just said sure, that was our first mistake.

Colby:"hey, you guys need any help with your bags?"

Mike:"nah, its cool bro we can manage"

Colby:"brooo's, I'm a professional let me take those bags off your hands"

Jack:"sure dude, what the hell its my B-day"

Colby:"seriously dude?"

Donny:"hell yeah my boy just turned twenty-one"

Colby:"congrats bro, lets get these to your room then lets celebrate"

 At that moment we should have known things were gonna get weird, but we were living in the moment. After making it to the room Colby told us about his side business as a drug dealer, we weren't new to a bong hit or two but we weren't tryna get high.

Colby:"dudes if y'all need anything just let me know, trees, pills, lines, lean etc etc, i'm your guy, oh yeah and I only have the best bud ever, crisis pack"

John Boy:"fuck yeah bro, I could go for a few joints"

Mike:"thats all you John Boy, i'm good"

Donny:"yeah…We are already high on life, heh heh.."

Colby:"come on dude's, don't be party poopers lets get fucked up for your boys birthday, lets smoke heavy crisis to the fucking face"

Jack:"i guess a little crisis won't hurt anyone"

Shawn:"bro are you sure, we don't even know this guy"

whispered Shawn to Jack

An awkward silence took over the room as everyone stared at me for my approval or disapproval, luckily an unknown voice from the hall broke the silence.

Unknown voice:"light bulb get back to work, theres some guys downstairs looking for you"

Colby:"sure thing dude, i'm just hanging with my bro's"

How we became his bro's?.....Yeah, none us knew the answer to that either, however we awkwardly tried to get rid of him and change the subject.

Jack:"how did you get a name like light bulb"

Yeah that was the only question that I could think of to change the subject, but it was his answer that would change the course of the next hour.

Colby:"my names Colby like so theres that"

Yeah that didn't make sense to us either, but theres more to his story...which also makes little sense.

Colby:"besides my name which is obvi"

"No Colby its not that obvi" I thought to myself.

Colby:"i'm like a bellhop in a bitching hotel, filled with rich people, so one day I was like...light bulb moment, I should sell drugs to the rich people at my hotel"

"Mhm yeah makes total sense now, why didn't I think of that" I get the feeling me and my bro's collectively thought.

Colby:"like I said guys if y'all need anything just let me know I gotta head out now might be a custy waiting"

At that moment we felt home free...We weren't, far from it

actually seeing as almost immediately after walking outside our room, gunshots ripped poor Colby to shreds, literally, as I stood in front of our open doorway I watched chunks of flesh and blood being torn away from his body as if he was in a blender, the sound was deafening, I stood there frozen, as everything moved around me in slow motion. Shawn ran into the bathroom, I guess he wanted to check his makeup before he died, John Boy hid behind a couch....Yeah, he's totally the genius of the group, Fyi...couches aren't bulletproof, Donny tackled me to the ground and landed on top of me, hashtag awkward, hashtag I crush puss so this isn't gay, hashtag why did he think us being on the ground would help us survive? Mike came through in the clutch he took action and did what any sane person would do, he ran and closed the door, which probably would have been enough to keep us out of whatever Colby was involved in any other time but sadly unknown voice guy relayed to these unknown shooters exactly what our best bud Colby told him which is we were Colby's bro's, I think you know what happens next, which would be good cause I don't, last thing I remember is a loud crash, the door swinging open and guys with mask running in. I'm guessing I was knocked unconscious, next thing I know i'm waking up in the back of a moving van with my bro's, sure we were banged up they got their licks in, but you really should see the other guys…Because there fine, so um, yeah.

Chapter 5: Sin Number 2
"Greed looks good on you"

After arriving god knows where the back doors of the van were opened, a guy threw in blacked out pillow cases for us and told us to put them on our heads we did what any group of tough guys would…We complied with their demands, after which they led us into what at the time sounded like a club and was later confirmed to be a club when the pillow cases were removed and we were in an office over looking a nightclub. Briefly left alone we quickly tried to figure out what was going on.

John Boy:"dudes what the fuck"

Shawn:"we're all gonna fucking die"

Mike:"fuck that, you can die if you want but i'm getting the fuck outta here!"

Donny:'no one is gonna die here, we're gonna get out of this"

John Boy:"get out of this? how the fuck are we gonna get out of this?"

Mike:"we wait till these mother fuckers come in here and we jump em"

Donny:"sounds like a plan to me"

Shawn:"sounds like a plan? where the fuck did you hear a plan?"

Mike:"I don't hear you coming up with any bright ideas"

Jack:"their right"

John Boy:"not you too"

Jack:"what else can we do? we don't have a choice"

Donny:"Jack's right we might as well die fighting if we're gonna die"

Shawn:"correction you mean i'm right, we're all gonna fucking die"

Panicking we scrambled to try and look around the office for anything we could use for a weapon, lets take a moment to run down what we thought were great weapon ideas while coming up with cool action packed catch phrases to over exaggerate the effectiveness of our weaponry. John Boy grabbed a mini metal trash can, lets just say "he'll be taking out the trash" Shawn grabbed a computer keyboard off the desk, I guess it was time to "Ctrl-Alt-Delete some assholes" Mike picked up a chair "to sit a mother fucker down" Donny grabbed a pair of scissors, guess he was ready to "cut through the bullshit" looking around with not many options left I grabbed a magazine "hashtag, paper cuts hurt like a bitch" armed to the teeth we stood tall ready for war. It was crunch time the door to the office opened up and in walked a man dressed in what can only be considered a cross between a leprechaun costume and a pimp suit, covered in tattoos and gold jewelry I couldn't help but think to myself "fucking bitching outfit bruh" sadly i'm guessing the shock of seeing this dude took the fight out of my bro's considering we all stood there holding our weapons of war waiting to see what would happen next. You probably figured out by now this is the second person we should have avoided yet couldn't, his name was Dice…No aka his parents literally named him Dice and basically he wanted to inform us on how Colby owed him fifty thousand dollars that for some reason we now owed…At that moment we were over joyed, you see a money problem is no problem at all when your parents are loaded, or so we thought.

Dice:" the fuck are you's standing around looking like you seen a ghost for? I haven't killed any of you's yet"

Donny:"listen dude you don't know who the fuck your messing with one phone call from me to my uncle and your a dead man"

Dice:"thanks for the advice tough guy, I guess I won't be letting you make any calls, any other geniuses amongst you?"

Mike:"maybe we can talk this out and make some kind of deal theres no reason why we can't forget any of this happened, we don't even know who you are"

Dice:"my names dice, nice to meet you, I bet your wondering how I got a name like Dice"

 "Oddly enough, yeah kinda" I thought to myself.

Dice:"you see my father wanted to name me, after all i'm his first born son, yet my mother wanted to name me after her father Robert who had just recently passed away before I was born. They decided a flip of a coin would decide the fate of my name, long story short my dad won but didn't have any names picked out, so seeing as he won the choice of my name gambling he decided to name me after something associated with gambling, hence "Dice" he also let me keep the quarter, still have it till this day.

"I mean, yeah but…Couldn't he just as easily named you slots or poker? Hell, he could have even been technical and named you coin toss" I thought to myself with a confused look on my face.

Dice:"but enough about me, i'm sure you lot want to know why your here"

"No sir we actually grown accustom to being here" Hashtag soooo obvi bro" I almost thought aloud.

Dice:"basically you lot owe me fifty thousand dollars your friend Colby couldn't seem to pay"

Shawn:"deal, great doing business with you"

John Boy:"what he said"

Mike:"yeah, its safe to assume he speaks for all of us right guys"

Donny:"certainly speaks for me"

Jack:"me too"

Dice:"wonderful, I like you guys, theres nothing more honorable then a man that pays his debts"

Jack:"sir, I've always felt the exact same thing, heh heh"

Dice:"sir? No need for formality call me Dice"

Jack:"ok Dice, would you like your money in check, money order or wire transfer?"

Dice:"cash"

Donny:"excellent choice, just point us to a bank, heck point us to an ATM"

Dice:"whats the rush guys? We got all night"

Mike:"definitely, its just that its our boys birthday"

Dice:"you don't say, well come on which of you is it?"

Jack:"that would be me, just turned 21"

Dice:"fuck we should celebrate"

Donny:"we don't want to impose, you seem like a busy man"

Dice:"nonsense, 21 is a special age we got to do this right, let me call up a couple of my girls, tonight we fuck, and feast...on drugs, you guys get fucked up right?"

John Boy:"yeah, I guess"

Mike:"Sure, a little"

Shawn:"definitely"

Donny:"um, sure"

Jack:"I guess we could"

Yeah, by girls he meant prostitutes and by get fucked up...He meant get fucked up, the next 30 minutes felt like a lifetime, we did more drugs in that half an hour then we ever did in our lives, that office looked like a scene out of a porn film, one big drug filled orgy, then I blacked out. When I woke up everyone was passed out except the most beautiful red head I had ever seen, who said three magic words even more beautiful then "I love you"

Red Head:"hey, lets go"

Jack:"um, sure…I just gotta get my bro's"

Red head:"hurry up, this asshole will kill you"

 After waking my bro's up, we quickly made our escape with this mysterious red head who would end up getting us into even more trouble.

Chapter 6: Sin Number 3
"Lust & what not"

Fast Forward past an awkward bus ride with a half naked stripper, we arrived at a rundown motel where our mystery heroine was living. Yup you guessed it, we followed her inside to see what other shenanigans the night had to offer. Our saviors name was Bella a stripper who works for Dice and just so happened to see us arriving at our hotel while she was in the lobby arguing with her sister who just so happened to be a maid at the hotel. As it turned out she was only stripping to make enough money to get out of Kroxce city to provide her sister with a better life and figured with our fifty grand, she could expedite that plan a bit.

Bella:"wheres the money?"

Jack:"money? What money?"

Bella:"don't play dumb with me, give me the money you were giving to Dice or I will call him and tell him where you are"

Donny:"and whats stopping us from just leaving before he even gets here?"

Thats when Bella pulled a gun from....god knows where, I mean she was literally wearing a bra, g-string and micro mini skirt, yet out came the biggest fucking revolver I had ever seen.

Bella:"this is what's fucking stopping you, any other dumb fucking questions?.....Good, now wheres the fifty grand?"

Mike:"look lets take it easy, you can have the fucking money just calm down"

Jack:"he's right the moneys yours, just stay calm"

Bella:"great, now that we are all on the same fucking page where the fuck, is the money?"

Now considering how unstable this chick seemed, telling her we never actually got the cash and didn't have it on us for her, wasn't an option, so I had to take charge, and think on my feet.

Jack:"its at our hotel"

Bella:"great, what the fuck are we waiting for? Lets go"

Flash forward past another very awkward bus ride and we were finally back at our hotel. This was the home stretch, all we had to do was pay this stripper, then head to the nearest airport and get out this crazy fucking city. Unfortunately, it wasn't gonna be that easy, the place was swarming with cops , turns out after theres a murder at a hotel, cops tend to wanna investigate, who knew? Now we were fucked, well kinda, you see Bella was crazy but not dumb, so she wasn't gonna march five hostages past a bunch of police officers, so she came up with the bright idea of staying outside with four of us, while one, went in to collect the money….That one, was yours truly, now I know your probably thinking to yourself what you would have done in a similar situation, but she had my bro's! I wasn't gonna risk any of their lives. Luckily the hotel had a casino, which even through all the chaos, was still fucking open! a simple wire transfer and like magic the cage clerk gave me a hundred grand in cash…What? You thought I wasn't gonna pay Dice? I might have been born that day, but I wasn't, born, that, day? you get the point. After heading out to pay Bella I asked her for a number I could reach Dice, she gave me the number, told us all to fuck off, and went on her merry way, I got on the phone with Dice and that call went a little something like this.

Dice:"Hello, who the fuck is this"

Jack:"um, jack the guy with the birthday"

Dice:"oh, Jack the dead man who owes me fifty grand and ran out on his debts"

Jack:"heh, about that, you see we kinda got kidnapped again while you were passed out, don't worry, we're safe now, I got you the money, and we can get it to you whenever an wherever you would like"

Dice:"where are you now?"

Jack:"back at the hotel"

Dice:"good stay there, I'll be there soon"

Totally wiped out, me and my bro's headed up to our room to leave the money and a note for Dice and grab our shit...I mean yeah, I was gonna pay him, but I never said I was dumb enough to do it in person.

Chapter 7: Sin Number 4
"Ex's & Envy"

 Turns out, our room was the center of the crime scene investigation, once again, who knew Kroxce detectives were so thorough? Matters got worse when I saw the lead detective, who just so happened to be my ex girlfriend, I know what your thinking, total fucking coincidence right? Not quite, see, my ex is the daughter of a big wig in the Federal Bureau of Investigations and it totally slipped my mind that 3 years ago when we broke up, it was because she had been offered a position in the vice unit in Kroxce city. Hooray everyone! its back to story time, my ex's name is Jessica, when we met I thought to myself,"Jack, Jessica, I'm hot, she's hot, perfect match right?" The 5 years age difference didn't matter, I was 18 dating a hot older woman, but things got complicated when she told me about her offer from vice, I don't know if she expected me to say something corny like,"don't go, stay here in my arms forever" or maybe,"where you go, I go, theres no way I could live apart from you" but what I actually said was,"fuck, i'm gonna miss you fe-bro" now for a brief intermission to explain our valley slang word of the day…"fe-bro" is a noun, used to describe your closest female bro's you know? Now that we established that, back to her, not, really, taking that response to well, telling me how much an asshole I was, and how she wished I was dead, yeah it was definitely a bad breakup to say the least, but here she was, the last person, I ever could have imagined running into, and the next person on my list of people I wish I could have avoided. What took place next, was a cross between, a witness interview, interrogation and lovers quarrel.

Jessica:"you boys look like shit, i'm guessing you been having a rough night"

Shawn:"you don't know the half of it"

Jack:"its good seeing you jess"

Jessica:"I can't say I feel the same"

Jack:"come on jess, don't tell me your still upset about…"

Jessica:"who said I was upset?"

Jack:"look, its been a long night, we're just trying to get out of this crazy ass town"

Jessica:"the nights not over yet boys, and as for leaving, ha, thats not gonna happen, your all suspects in a drug related homicide…Now, why don't you guys tell me how a known drug dealer, connected to one of this city's most dangerous drug kingpins, ends up dead in front of your hotel room? Or, how you guys end up alive and well, after being reportedly kidnaped by the gunmen?"

Mike:"wait what? Suspects?"

Donny:"we had nothing to do with this"

Jack:"relax guys, she's just kidding"

Jessica:"oh really, you guys are under arrest"

John Boy:"you can't arrest us, on what grounds?"

Jessica:"to be determined, but I can hold you for up to 36 hours, so get used to this face boys"

 And like that, we were handcuffed, escorted out the hotel, placed in separate squad cars, and taken off to the police station.

After arriving at the police station, I was placed in a cell with a drunk who believed he was the reincarnation of Nyarah, hashtag, why me. I never got the guys name, so, lets just call him Drunk Nyarah, our conversation went a little something like this.

Drunk Nyarah:"what are you in for my child?"

Jack:"i'm a witness"

Drunk Nyarah:"oh, and what have you witnessed my son? That I may know the ill's of this world"

Jack:"sorry, but i don't understand"

Drunk Nyarah:"you were put here to bare witness to

Sedeneves wickedness, for judgment day is upon the earth"

Jack:"um, ok…Well, I saw a man get killed in front of me, and then I was kidnapped, drugged, and I think sexually violated, then I escaped, only to be held at gunpoint and extorted, while my best friends were held hostage"

Drunk Nyarah:"I see, my child…well, godspeed, its time for my nap"

Jack:"huh ?"

And that was my blasphemous conversation with drunk Nyarah, his advice…Godspeed? What the fuck kind of Nyarah!!!….Not long after that, I was brought into an interrogation room where I would try once again to plead my case to Jessica.

Jessica:"so, you ready to talk"

Jack:"I have been ready to talk, but your not listening, i'm the victim here"

Jessica:"your the victim, thats rich, I thought we had something, and in the end you showed me what we had meant nothing to you"

Jack:"wait, what?"

Thats, when I realized I was right, she was in fact still upset about the break up, and me and my bro's were only being held prisoner out of spite, hashtag, what a bitch.

Jack:"jess, please don't tell me this is about us, I have literally been through some fucked up shit tonight, hell, theres a crazy, drug dealing pimp, probably still looking forward to killing me, I don't have time for these games, so, if your still so broken up about our breakup, lets fuck already and make up, other than that I want a fucking lawyer, a phone call, and I want my fucking bro's"

So um, yeah, we totally fucked in the interrogation room, but this isn't one of those kind of stories where I go into detail and say shit like,"she ran into my arms wanting me to take her, in all the ways that only I could, I ripped off her clothes like a savage dog, trying to get at a piece of meat, only to throw her onto the desk and thrust into her, in that moment, fully connected, eye to eye, she knew, she was mine" so lets fast forward past that bit, shall we? Winded after, you know? We finally got to talk like rational adults.

Jessica:"fuck, I needed that"

Jack:"me to, tonights been hell, its good to have one good thing, one ray of light in all this fucked up darkness"

Jessica:"you think i'm a ray of light?"

Jack:"of course jess, I know you think I'm an asshole but I really did care about you"

Everything was going perfect, me and Jesica were reconnecting, me and my bro's were together again, but before we could leave the police station, in walks a detective with a very familiar red head. Turns out Bella's sister was dating Colby, so when detectives went to question the mystery maid, they got pretty suspicious when they realized her sister was Dice's main girl, the fact she was arrested with fifty thousand dollars on her didn't help either. Now, things could have still worked out, if only she didn't see me and call out.

Bella:"babe"

Jessica:"babe? do you know that girl"

Jack:"never seen her in my life, heh, heh"

Bella:"babe, tell these assholes your the one who gave me the money"

Jessica:"she really seems to think she knows you"

Jack:"listen, to be honest, she's just a crazy fucking stripper that helped us escape Dice, then she robbed us"

Jessica:"you see, its lies like that...just go, get the fuck out of here!!!"

 Trust me, she didn't have to tell me twice. After calling a cab, we waited outside in front of the police station, not long after, out came Bella, who was being released since they couldn't tie her to anything, one awkward chat later she was gone, again.

Bella:"if you tell the cops anything about me, i'll fucking kill you"

Shawn:"definitely"

John Boy:"wouldn't blame you"

Mike:"ok"

Donny:"sure, thing"

Jack:"yes ma'am"

 Yes ma'am? yeah, I was out of it, all I wanted was to head back to the safety of the burbs.

Bella:"great, now fuck off"

 Like a whirl wind, she was in and out of our lives once again, just in time when our cab pulled up.

Chapter 8: Sin Number 5

"Wrath on the way"

This next bit of crazy was brief, but very intricate to what inevitably would happen by the end of the night. Our cab drivers name was Brandon, aka The Hog, this fine upstanding gentleman could only be described as a greasy, sweaty trailer park delinquent, who just so happened to be an ex con, and obsessed with Bella to whom he's a customer. You get the gist, he rolls up, seeing us talking to his girl, we get into his van not knowing theres an issue, and yeah, shenanigans ensued.

The Hog:"so, where you guys going?"

John boy:"just take us somewhere we can eat"

Shawn:"yeah, i'm starving"

Donny:"we should go straight to the airport"

Mike:"D-notes right, lets not take anymore risk"

John Boy:"its gonna take awhile before the jets up and running, we might as well catch our breath and get something to eat"

The Hog:"kinda need you guys to decide"

Jack:"food...take us wherever theres food"

Donny:"are you sure bro?"

Jack:"yeah lets eat, what else could possibly happen"

Boy was I wrong, as we started driving it became clear that our cab driver had something on his mind.

The Hog:"I noticed a girl with you guys when I pulled up, she didn't need a ride?"

Donny:"fuck her"

The Hog:"fuck her? I'm guessing y'all had a falling out"

Mike:"a falling out is a understatement"

Shawn:"lets just say we never, wanna fucking see her again"

The Hog:"did any of you fuck her?"

John Boy:"what?"

The Hog:"did any of you cocksuckers fuck her"

Donny:"who the fuck do you think your talking to"

The Hog:"a bunch of dead piss ants if any of you fucked my Bella"

thinking back to the orgy that took place in Dice's office...Yup, I definitely fucked his Bella, we kinda all did. Realizing how volatile the situation was, I decided to do what we should have done when we encountered the first lunatics of the night. I jumped out the fucking car….Thats right, no hesitation, no questions asked, I jumped out a moving car, because I refused to be held hostage, threatened, held at gunpoint or any other fucked up shit. As my body bounced off the cement and rolled along the street, all I could think was,"why couldn't I have just stayed home for my birthday? Maybe watched a movie and order some take-out" but after the tumbling stopped and I laid in the road coughing up blood, I could see the car stop and my bro's hop out to help me and I thought to myself,"i love you bro's, hashtag R.I.P me, hashtag I better be fucking missed" then I passed out.

When I came to, I was in a diner…yeah, a fucking diner, not an emergency room, where people mainly end up after a near fatal accident, instead my boys decide a diner would suffice, hashtag I feel the love.

Chapter 9: Sin Number 6
"No Guts, No Gluttony?"

After my boys filled me in of what took place after I passed out, I realized that it was just dumb luck I happened to hop out the cab right in front of a diner. Covered in bruises, dirty, with ripped and torn clothes, we all looked like shit, but we were alive, and for the first time that night, we just, started laughing, I don't know if it was to keep from crying, or perhaps we all went fucking nuts, but we were just happy to be alive. It wasn't long until a waitress came by who would end up further sealing our fates, her name was Gypsy, an adorable self proclaimed fortune teller and Mayalita…Yeah, nuts, I felt the same way, but sadly she was exactly what the doctor ordered, a cute blonde with a nice personality, and the comedic gold of letting her read our fortunes, we ate, and laughed, and she was seriously the most normal person we had met that whole night. That was, until she got to my fortune, you see, she told us all that we would go off on some journey or whatever, and change the world, acquire riches beyond our wildest dreams, and become krowlocks, the only catch was one of us had to die...And the person, was gonna be me. My response went a little like this.

Jack:"your fucking insane"

Gypsy:"its true, if you stay on this path you will die before the night is up, and your death will change all of your destiny's forever"

Jack:"well, good thing i'm getting the fuck off this path, lets go guys"

Gypsy:"you can't run from fate"

Jack:"watch me, check please"

Mike:"wait bro maybe if…"

Jack:"if what? lets fucking go!!!"

Mike:"if we find out how though, can't we avoid it?"

Jack:"find out how? this bitch is crazy! not psychic"

Shawn:"then why are you so scared?"

Jack:"i'm not scared, she just reminded me how much we really should get out of this city before we do actually end up dead, have you all forgot about Dice?"

Gypsy:"Dice? the pimp?"

Jack:"great, of course you would know him"

Gypsy:"I don't know him, per say, but my friends sister works for him"

 "Don't say it, please, don't say it" is what I thought to myself before she said it.

Gypsy:"her names Bella, me and her sister have been friends for years she's a maid at…"

Jack:"yeah, we know where she's a maid at, which is why we really must be going"

Mike:"yeah lets go"

Donny:"thanks for the food, it was great we just got prior engagements"

Shawn:"thanks for everything"

John Boy:"bye bye now"

Gypsy:"and how are you going to get there?"

Jack:"get where?"

Gypsy:"exactly, your phones busted from your fall, and the rest of your phones are dead"

Jack:"and you know that how exactly?"

Gypsy:"duh, psychic remember?"

She was right, but it had to be a lucky guess, right?

Gypsy:"look, I can drive you to the hotel, you have money there right? And other shit you might need? Besides, my friends probably getting off work, and I usually pick her up anyway"

Something told me to just refuse her offer, hell, we could have been better off hitch hiking, but I simply wanted to get this night over with as fast as possible, so I agreed, big mistake. On the way to the hotel as Gypsy sped like a maniac, she told us about how she became a fortune teller and Mayalita…Which, ultimately only confirmed she was bat shit crazy. According to her she used to work at the hotel but was fired for stealing food from the room service trays she was assigned to bring to guests….Yeah, bat shit, in fact she claimed the only reason she became a waitress is so she could eat the left over food that would be thrown out…..Hashtag, what the fuck, hashtag, gross, hashtag, way to much information. Trust me, it gets better, she went on to further explain how the reason for her appetite was because of a curse that was put on her by a guest who stayed at the hotel a year earlier, what was this curse you ask? and why was she cursed? Turns out, Gypsy, was a free loading thief, and one day her and her friend decided to swipe a guest credit card info so they could rent out the pent house suit for a day of ill gotten bliss, that guest was a Papalito, who cursed the two girls, since the girls wanted to eat and live off of the suffering of other as thieves, they would need to make amends eating the scraps of others and spending their lives in service of others, if not they would embody their inner nature, the Papalito told Gypsy her inner nature was rotten to the core, so if she didn't comply, she would rot on the outside and be forced to feed on the dead flesh of others....Zombies? Hashtag, yeah she said this shit. Back to the story, her friend was told that she was a leech at heart, too proud to work for her own in life, and if she didn't comply she would be forced to live off the blood of others…Vampires? Hashtag, whatever medication she's on should be illegal. Pulling up to the hotel all I could think about was getting my shit, and heading to the airport, I just had to stay alive a little while longer.

Chapter 10: Sin Number 7
"Power & Pride"

Quickly me and my boys headed up to our room to get our shit, by that time the cops had cleared out, Gypsy insisted on following behind us onto the elevator, but at the time we were so focused we didn't even care to find out why. When the elevator door opened, something told me that something was off, but in my mind we were moments away from being able to leave this city, so after a deep breathe we started walking down the hall to our room. A calm before the storm could describe how we felt during that walk, it was like walking in slow motion, by the time we got to the door, my life had fully flashed before my eyes, memories of my bro's, and our life brought a smile to my face. Then the door opened, and that smile vanished when I saw Dice, Bella and her mysterious sister the maid, Gypsy called out to her friend, who's name is Ruby while rushing over to her, Bella tried calming them down, by telling them everything would be alright, even though she seemed more afraid then they did, me and my bro's were at gunpoint once again, as four of Dices bodyguards surrounded us, closing the door behind us and blocking off any chance for escape, we're fucked…At that point I didn't feel

like I had any luck left, I thought of
my fortune, and came to grips with
the fact that I was gonna die, but I
refused to let anything happen to
my bro's.

Jack:"I can get you your money if
thats what your after, just let my
friends go, all you need is one of
us"

Dice:"money? You think this is
about, money? You rich kids, with
your daddies trust fund money,
think you can do whatever you
want, and get out of any situation
with money"

Jack:"listen, I had a long fucking
night, so seriously, if you want
money, I can get it, if not, I guess

your gonna fucking kill me right asshole? So get it the fuck over with, just don't ruin this face, I kinda want an open casket"

Dice:"since when did this guy grow some balls? Do the rest of you feel the same?"

My bro's looked at me, and i could tell by their eyes, they were ready to die along side me, but thats not what I wanted, so before they could speak.

Jack:"I speak for myself fucktard, no one else here needs to be involved, hell, if you have your bitches drop the guns, me and you could settle this like men" the energy in the room shifted, I was no longer afraid, I was just pissed the fuck off, my boys had started to calm down as well, and even though my words seemed to initially piss Dice off he seemed to calm down as well.

Dice:"relax kid, i'm not gonna kill you or your friends all I want is my money, if i did want you dead, I would have just sent my men to kill you"

Mike:"like my boy said, money isn't a problem we can get you whatever you need"

Dice:"thats good to know…as for you"

Without warning Dice pulled his gun and shot Bella in the head, the moments after that are a haze, after the gunshot my stomach sank, I couldn't hear anything but my own breathing and the faint sound of Bellas sister crying over her body. Before I could think, Bellas sister was running over to Dice enraged over the death of her sister, shots rang out, from which direction or from who, I couldn't tell you, all I know, is Bellas sister was shot down before ever reaching Dice, Gypsy attempted to run, she almost got by me before she was shot, her blood sprayed from her body, covering my face before she fell to the ground, I don't know why, but I looked at my Brothers, and decided that I had to save them anyway I could, before I could think about it, my body just moved, almost instantly I was on top of Dice wrestling him for his gun…And then, bang. My body felt weak, my chest was so warm, I watched Dice get up from the ground but couldn't do the same, I was just so tired, my bro's were screaming but I couldn't hear them, all I could do is watch as they were dragged away by Dices men, then everything went black.

Hashtag, death is a real bitch!!! hashtag, definitely, don't try it at home kids, laying in a dark room I could see a light in the distance that moved closer to me as the seconds past until I was suddenly awake, my body felt like it was on fire, and a girl was holding my head on her lap and crying over me, her tears were so cold running down my face, when my eyes were finally able to focus I realized it was Ruby, Bellas sister. Some how I made it to my feet, I tried asking Ruby what was going on, but she wouldn't speak, she just grabbed my arm and led me to the elevator, once inside she looked at me and spoke for the first time.

Ruby:"you wanna save your friends don't you?"

Jack:"fuck yeah"

Ruby:"follow me and you will"

Jack:"how are we…?"

Ruby:"does it matter how?"

Jack:"no, it doesn't"

Ruby:"all that matters is you have the power to save your friends, and kill Dice"

For some reason, I just knew she was right, even though I was in pain, I felt, different, powerful, when the elevator doors opened the lobby was filled with police and detectives heading upstairs, we managed to head out unseen thanks to all the chaos, however as we were exiting the hotel my ex Jessica was entering, she grabbed my arm, and Ruby grabbed her by the throat, and with one simple request from Ruby she agreed to drive us anywhere we wanted to go, I've never seen anything like it, it was like Jessica was hypnotized and would obey anything Ruby commanded. Not soon after we were on the road, speeding to Dices club, a car sped up and crashed into us from behind, causing our car to flip over. All I could smell was blood, Jessica was upside down hanging in her seat by her seatbelt, Ruby was ejected from the car, and I was in a pool of blood and glass, after crawling out of one of the cars windows, I freed Jessica and dragged her out the car, she was passed out but still alive, thats when Ruby called out to me from the other side of the car where she was face to face with our attacker.

The Hog was back, he was stalking Bella at the time Dice grabbed her and followed Dice to the hotel, for some strange reason he got it in his head her death was somehow on me.

The Hog:"you fucking Xinner, you got my precious Bella killed, now i'm gonna kill you"

Ruby:"Xinner, I like that, show this asshat how much of a Xinner you really are"

I stood there, faking confusion, I knew exactly what she wanted me to do, and I couldn't help but want to as well, I looked in her eyes and saw bloodlust, and I look at him and saw food. Memories of what took place after I was shot started to come back to me, the feeling of Rubys teeth piercing my skin, the rush of my blood flowing out of me into her, the feeling of total bliss being at the center of her universe, it was a feeling better then sex, so yeah, the bitch bit me and I kinda liked it. There was no turning back, my brothers needed me and this asshole was the only thing standing in my way of getting to them. I let my instincts guide me, within the blink of an eye I was behind him with my back to his, the scent of blood strong in the air, I looked down only to realize I had his heart in my hands, with the effort it takes to twitch or move a finger, I cleared a distance of at least 12 feet, ripped a mans heart out, and did it all in the blink of an eye, I didn't even feel myself move. The scent of blood started to take over my being, I turned to his dying, bleeding body to feast on this sweet nectar that poured from his chest, but before I could I was stoped by Ruby, she explained that I was only in transition and if I was to feed I would be cursed to live as a monster for eternity, but if I didn't I would die after this parasitic virus consumed me and my soul would remain pure. I decided to walk the path of the light, all that mattered was saving my brothers, after that I could die happily. We got into The Hogs car which wasn't as banged up as Jessicas, and took off leaving her there in hopes that someone would get her some help, as we drove, I started to think back on all of the goals and dreams me and my brothers had and how I wasn't going to be able to see any of those dreams come true, but in my heart I was at peace, I knew I was making the right choice, and Ruby agreed.

Ruby:"your making the right choice you know?"

Jack:"I know, but it doesn't make it any easier"

Ruby:"trust me you don't want this life"

Jack:"you seem to be doing ok"

Ruby:"your wrong, I spent the last year trying not to kill and eat the closest people to me, including my own sister"

Jack:"so who'd you eat?"

Ruby:" who'd I eat? You don't get it do you? I didn't eat anyone, I have lived with this curse using supplements and eating foods rich in iron to keep my blood count up so this parasite wouldn't kill me"

Jack:"wait what? can't I do the same thing?"

Ruby:"maybe, but those powers of yours come at a price, to use them you increase your own blood flow and speed up the process of your death, I ate ravenously and took more supplements then was humanly possible, but I was still weak all the time and hungry for what this thing inside me truly wanted which is blood"

Jack:"so after I kill Dice I just gotta go on a special diet"

Ruby:"listen, I'm just trying to be honest with you, if you want to live exit the car go on your diet and live as long as you can, but if you go up against Dice and his men you will die, wether by the parasite or a bullet and because your still human a bullet will kill you, just like it almost killed me, feeding on your blood was the only way I could live, as I fed on you I saw into your past and realized how much you cared about your friends thats why I gave you my blood, to give you the chance to use this curse for revenge"

Jack:"their not my friends, we're brothers"

Ruby:"my bad, lets go save your brothers"

Jack:"fuck yeah"

 We pulled up to an alley leading to a side entrance of Dices club, I could smell fear and blood in the air, my anger took over me, I ran towards the side entrance and ripped the door from its frame, two of Dices guards stood there shocked for a split second, before I tore their heads from their bodies, by the time Ruby made it to the entrance I was already inside the club wreaking havoc, after killing a few guards and blood spraying on patrons, panic filled the club, the screams of club goers over powered the crap music being played and finally Dices men knew something was up, which is exactly what I wanted, killing these assholes was a little too easy, so I welcomed the challenge. I let the club clear out, after all,

this fight was between me and
Dice, I stood in the center of the
club surrounded by Dices goons
armed to the teeth, but I felt no
fear, just excitement about how
much I would enjoy killing them
all, they fired shots, hundreds of
rounds rushed towards me in slow
motion,I stood there and thought
to myself all the ways I would like
to kill them, but for the sake of
time, I decided to just make things
quick, I simply grabbed the bullets
once they were in arms reach and
threw them back at who fired
them, I thought killing them with
their own weapons was poetic in a
way, before they knew what was
happening they were being
shredded with their own
ammunition. as the smoke of gun
fire cleared I headed up to Dices
office, before opening the door
Ruby ran through the club and
grabbed my hand, I already knew
why, I could smell the blood, the
scent was too thick to be from

being beaten up, my brothers were either dead or dying on the other side of that door.

Ruby:"wait, I can take things from here"

Jack:"its fine, I need to see for myself"

Ruby:"but…."

Jack:"but what? trust me i'm fine"

 I wasn't fine, I was scared to death to see what happened to my brothers in that room, but I owed it to them to be the one to kill Dice, so I opened the door. My brothers laid dying on the floor like animals as Dice sat at his desk smoking a cigar with two of his guards at his side, so much rage was inside me I couldn't bring myself to lay a finger on Dice out of fear that whatever I did wouldn't be the most perfect way of killing him leaving me unsatisfied, so I commanded his men to kill him, the look of confusion on his face, the laughter that almost escaped his mouth before the burning sensation of bullets entering his chest, before he heard a thing or saw his men draw their weapons he was shot, coughing up and drowning on his own blood, the look on his face was priceless, I commanded his men to put their guns to their heads and kill themselves, which they did without hesitation, Dice died moments later. I stood over my brothers with tears in my eyes, I could hear their hearts slowing, and sensed their lives slipping away, there was only one thing I could do.

Ruby:"don't do it, I know what your thinking"

Jack:"so you read minds now?"

Ruby:"I don't have to read minds to know what you're thinking, but what you're not thinking about, is what they would want"

Jack:'they're my brothers, I know exactly what they would want"

In that moment she knew, I had fully made up my mind to spend an eternity cursed alongside my brothers, I released my fangs like twin katanas, and plunged them deep into the throats of my brothers one after the other, drinking what little blood they had left, and leaving just enough for the virus inside my blood to spread after pouring it from my wrist into their mouths.

Donny:'what the hell?"

Ruby:"trust me your not in hell yet"

Mike:" how is this possible"

Jack:"I brought you assholes back, now enough questions"

Shawn:"i'm not dead, so yeah, fuck the questions guys"

John Boy:"or maybe we are dead?"

Jack:"nobody is dead nobody is gonna die, Fuck!!! last time I do anything for you ungrateful shits"

Mike:"you saved us? Bro, thank…."

Jack:"don't fucking say it, I didn't do this for thanks, I did it cause…"

Donny:"we're bros, he did it cause we're bros"

We all stood around awkwardly trying not to cry or hug each other, until finally I couldn't take it, and so I cried out.

Jack:"I FUCKING LOVE YOU BRO'S!!!!"

 We all ran into each others arms for a group hug, but we were all so drained we ended up falling to the ground. Crying in silence we all laid back on the floor looking up at the ceiling. Finally we just took a breathe and realized the night was finally fucking over. I explained to my brothers I was cursed but they had a choice, without hesitation they walked over and drank from Dices corpse, sealing their fates with mine. Ruby began to leave, I tried to stop her, but she had her own shit she wanted to sort out.

Jack:"Ruby wait"

Ruby:"for what? the deed is done, the bitch is dead"

Jack:"stay with me, I don't know anything about being a vampire"

Ruby:"vampire? hahaha, your a real idiot aren't you?"

Jack:"what do you mean?"

Ruby:"this isn't a fucking movie, or some Nikolaus James Breland novel. This is real fucking life and what we are….is so fucking worse than a vampire"

Jack:"what are we?"

Ruby:"I don't have all the answers, thats what i'm going to go find out, all I know is our kind are connected to some artifact called Nagfall, I never found out what it was just that vampire mythology was based on our species and that by comparison, vampires are house pets"

 After that she turned and left, I didn't know what this life had in store for me, but I was happy to be alive. Six days later I started writing this, and yeah, these last six days have been fucking crazy, spoiler alert, book two? hint hint, way wilder then book one, I know what your saying, hashtag, impossible, hashtag, The West End Boyz volume one rules, but I guess you just gotta stay tuned to find out.

Outro-duction? "To be fucking continued"

So what have we learned? never go to Kroxce city unless your looking to die or become undead, always have your bros backs, especially when their your closest bros, most times your ex just wants to fuck, red headed strippers are a problem, the killer is always the hotel maid, fyi, Dice shot me but technically the maid killed me, oh, here's a good one, fuck fortune tellers, hashtag I'd rather be surprised, did Shawn ever get laid? Find out next time on The West End Boyz volume 2, will John Boy ever get any more lines of dialogue, once again theres another book coming people, and last but not least we learned, "The West End Boyz fucking rocks!!!".